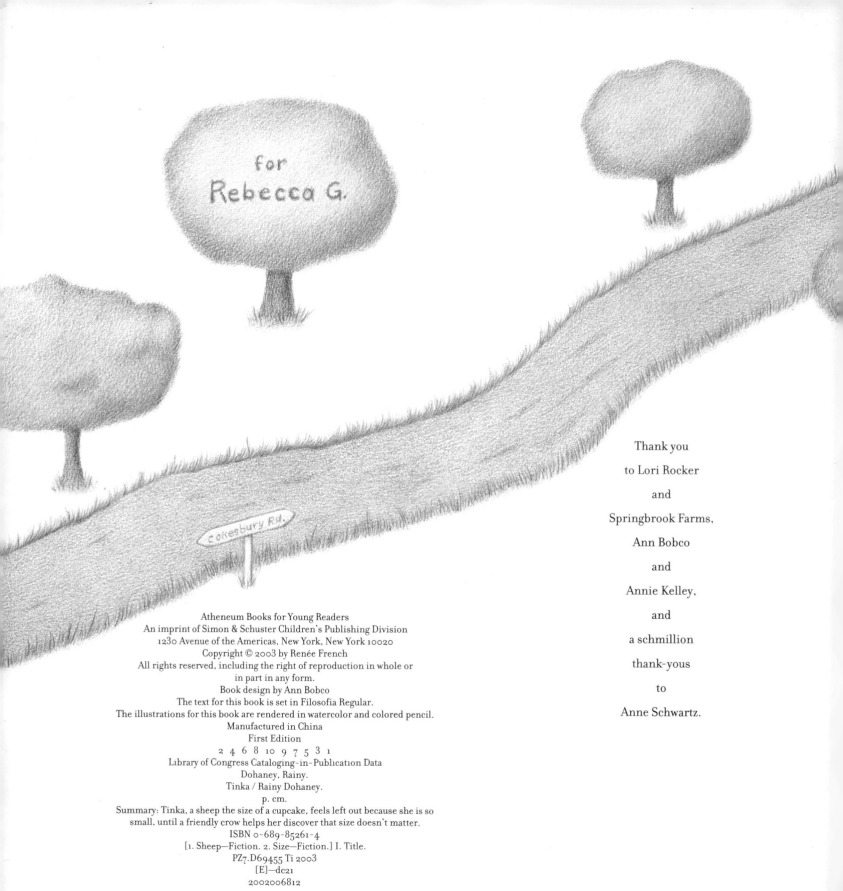

for
Rebecca G.

Cokesbury Rd.

Atheneum Books for Young Readers
An imprint of Simon & Schuster Children's Publishing Division
1230 Avenue of the Americas, New York, New York 10020
Copyright © 2003 by Renée French
All rights reserved, including the right of reproduction in whole or
in part in any form.
Book design by Ann Bobco
The text for this book is set in Filosofia Regular.
The illustrations for this book are rendered in watercolor and colored pencil.
Manufactured in China
First Edition
2 4 6 8 10 9 7 5 3 1
Library of Congress Cataloging-in-Publication Data
Dohaney, Rainy.
Tinka / Rainy Dohaney.
p. cm.
Summary: Tinka, a sheep the size of a cupcake, feels left out because she is so
small, until a friendly crow helps her discover that size doesn't matter.
ISBN 0-689-85261-4
[1. Sheep—Fiction. 2. Size—Fiction.] I. Title.
PZ7.D69455 Ti 2003
[E]—dc21
2002006812

Thank you

to Lori Rocker

and

Springbrook Farms,

Ann Bobco

and

Annie Kelley,

and

a schmillion

thank-yous

to

Anne Schwartz.

TINKA

by

Rainy Dohaney

AN ANNE SCHWARTZ BOOK • Atheneum Books for Young Readers

New York London Toronto Sydney Singapore

Down at the end of Cokesbury Road there was a quiet old place called McEwen's Farm. Farmer McEwen had five sheep:

Myla,

Melda,

Nyla,

Welda, and . . .

Tinka, who happened to be the smallest sheep
anyone in those parts had ever seen.

She was the size of a cupcake.

Once a year all the sheep would line up for shearing. The big sheep would produce a huge fleece of wool, enough to make a basketful of yarn.

But Tinka's fleece made only enough yarn to
knit a tiny sweater fit for a hamster, or an egg cozy.

At night when it was time to sleep, all the sheep lay together in their bed of hay—all but Tinka, who slept in her own little bed in the corner of the barn.

"Can't I sleep with the rest of you guys?" she'd beg. "I'm a sheep too!"

"No, Teensy Tinka, you're too small. We'd surely squish you," the others would answer.

And that's when Tinka would feel so alone that she'd
cry herself to sleep.

But Tinka DID have one friend—

Sooty, the crow.

He always knew how to make Tinka laugh.

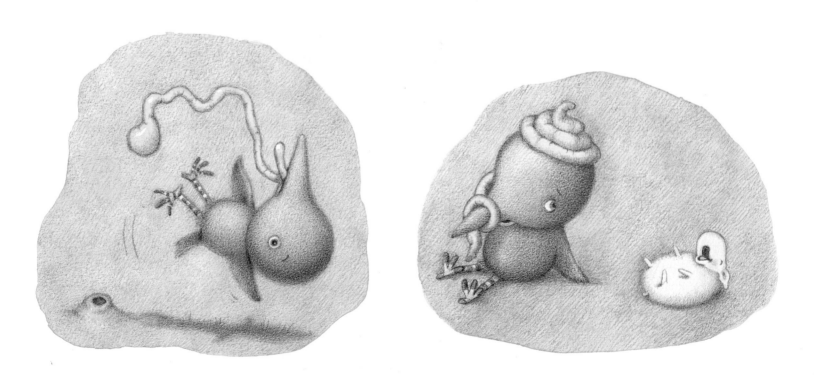

Every year on the faraway hill, a huge purple spider would appear. And every year the sheep would celebrate because it meant that spring had arrived. As the days and the grass grew longer, they'd imagine what it would be like to visit the spider—though they knew that was impossible. After all, neither Myla nor Melda, Nyla nor Welda could get over Farmer McEwen's fence.

Poor Tinka wasn't even tall enough to SEE the spider.

"Oh, please tell me,
what does he look like?"
she asked the sheep
one spring morning.

"He's baah-aah-
aah-eeootiful!"
baah-ed Myla.

"And gigaah-
aah-aah-antic!"
maah-ed Welda.

"Too bad you're
too small to see him,"
snorted Melda.

"Yeah, it's too baah-aah-aad you're too small,"
Nyla joined in while the others laughed.

"It's not funny," Tinka said under her breath, as she stood
on a pebble, on her tiptoes, stretching to see just a tiny speck
of spider. But as much as she tried she couldn't see a thing.

Just then Sooty came in for a rough landing.

"Whoa. Sorry, kid," he said.

"Hey Sooty, can you see the purple spider from up there?"
Tinka asked.

"I sure can, pal," Sooty answered. "When I fly I can see for
a schmillion miles."

"I wish I could see him too," Tinka said, all dreamy-eyed.
"Or visit!

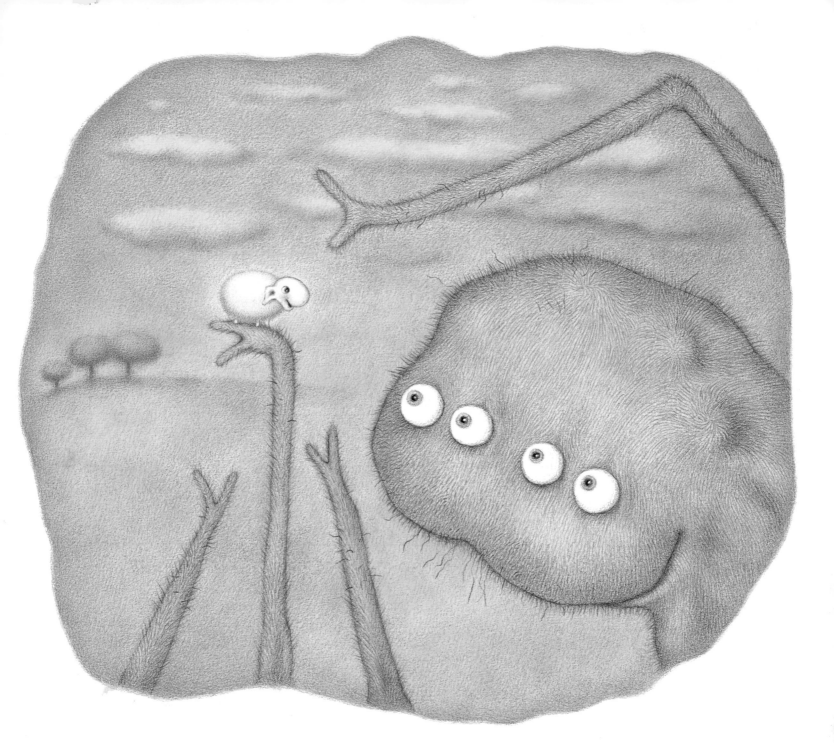

"Why, if I could visit him, I'd trot right up and tell him he's the most spectacular spider in the whole world."

Then she sighed. "Too bad I'm too little. I could never even get past the chicken coop."

"Little, schmittle," replied Sooty.
He scratched his wing. He looked
at his feet.

"Well, I guess I'll just have to
check out Mr. Spider myself," he said
at last, and he took a running start,

and launched himself into the air.

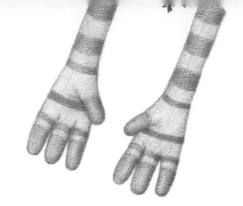

"Hey!" Tinka called.
Without a thought,
she leaped as high
as she could after
her friend.
"Take me with you!
I'm small enough
for you to carry me!"

"If you insist," Sooty said, swooping back down.
"Hop aboard, kid, and hold on to your hooves!"

Up, up, and up, the two friends flew, until they were so high the barn looked tiny and the sheep looked tinier.

The fields spread before them like Tinka's quilt back home.
"I feel bigger than the biggest sheep there ever was!" she cried.

And then she saw
him, all huge and
purple and dancing
in the wind. Right below
Tinka was the spider,
and the other sheep
were right—he WAS
baah-aah-aah-eeootiful.

But the closer they flew, the less
he looked like one big spider,

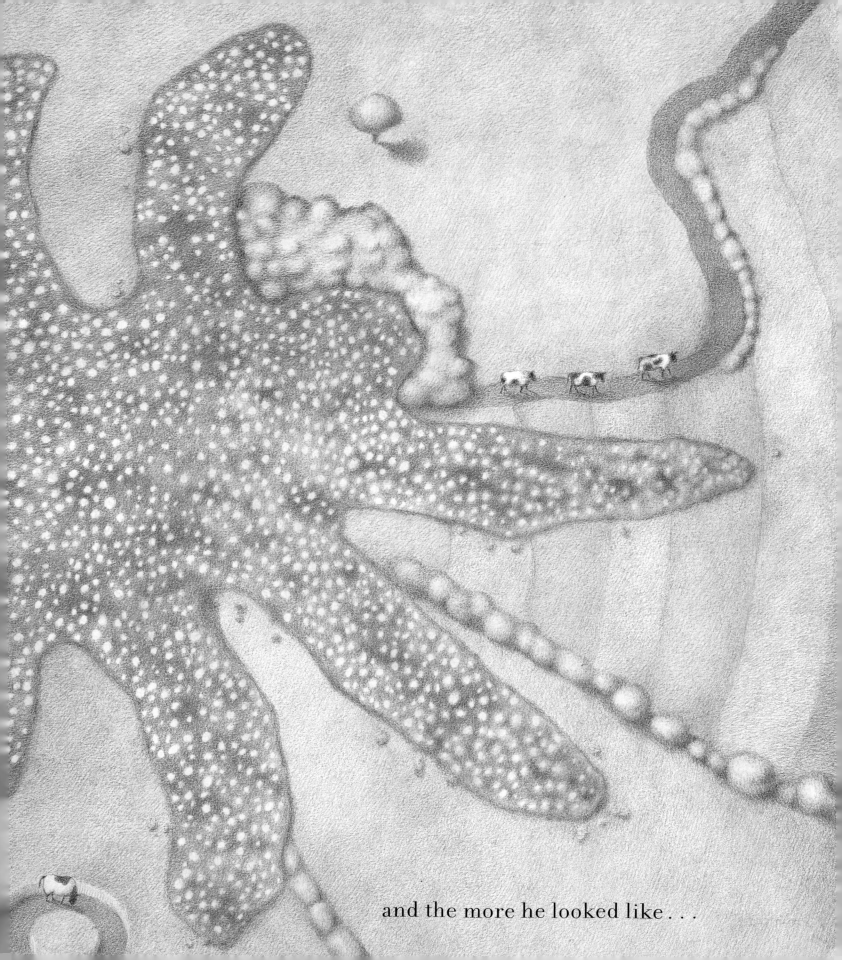

and the more he looked like . . .

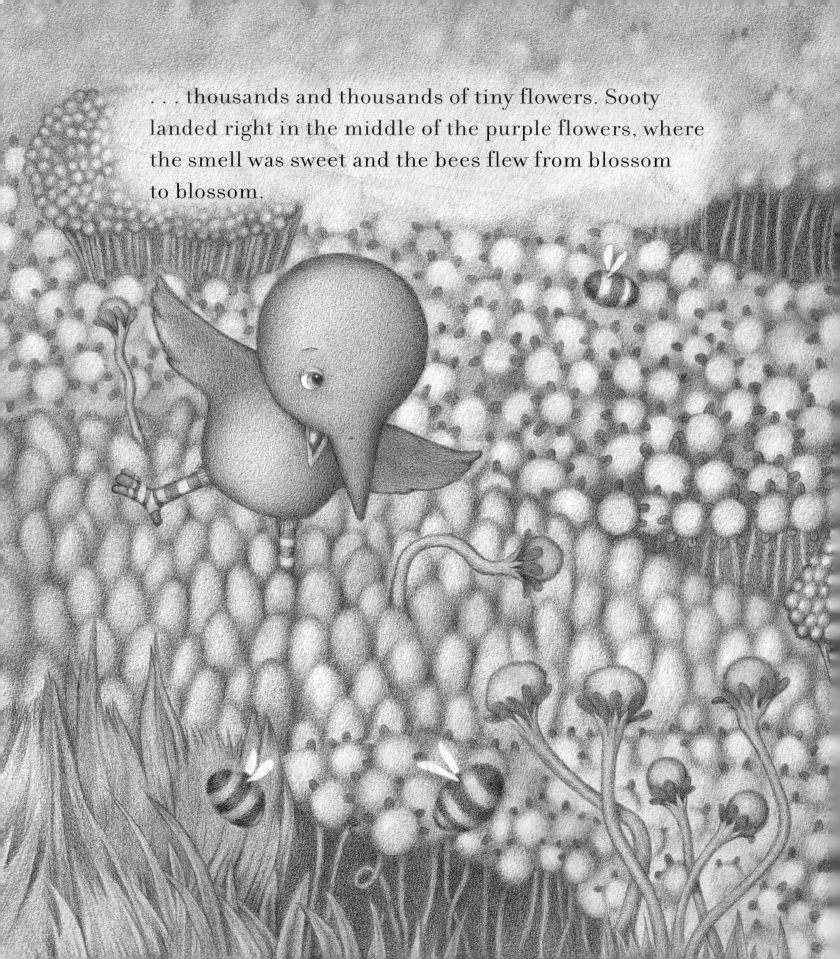

. . . thousands and thousands of tiny flowers. Sooty landed right in the middle of the purple flowers, where the smell was sweet and the bees flew from blossom to blossom.

"Hey, this isn't a spider at all!" Tinka shouted.
"Wait till I tell those silly sheep."

Back at the farm the others were starting to wonder where Tinka had gone.

"Look, her little bed is empty," Myla noticed.

"She probably raah-aah-an away," Melda suggested.

"Oh no, I hope it wasn't something I said," whined Welda.

"Nobaah-aah-dy ever listens to you anyway," muttered Nyla.

In the spider field Sooty and Tinka were having a
wonderful time.

"Hey, Sooty, I'm the world's only flying sheep,"
Tinka laughed.

After a long day at play Tinka started to get tired.
"I might need to go home," she said.
"Sure thing, kid," Sooty agreed.
He made her a delicate crown of purple flowers,
picked her up, and together they took off once again.

As they passed over the quilty fields, Tinka realized that
she was looking forward to the comfort of her own bed.

They landed next to the barn, and Tinka
thanked her best friend for the amazing ride.

Then she snuck under the barn door . . . and tiptoed
past the big sheep, who were just nodding off to sleep.

Myla was the first to hear the little hoofsteps, and she whispered, "Is that you, Teensy Tinka?"

"Yes, it's me. I'm baah-aah-ack from a trip to see the purple spider," Tinka whispered, holding back a giggle.

"The purple spider!" All four sheep sat right up and eyed her excitedly.

"How on earth did you get there?"

"Was it scary?"

"Why don't you sleep here with us and tell us all about it?"

"We'll be careful not to squish you."

But Tinka only smiled and politely said, "I'll tell you everything in the morning."

Then she headed off to her corner of the barn.

Her little bed was cozy and warm, and best of all . . .

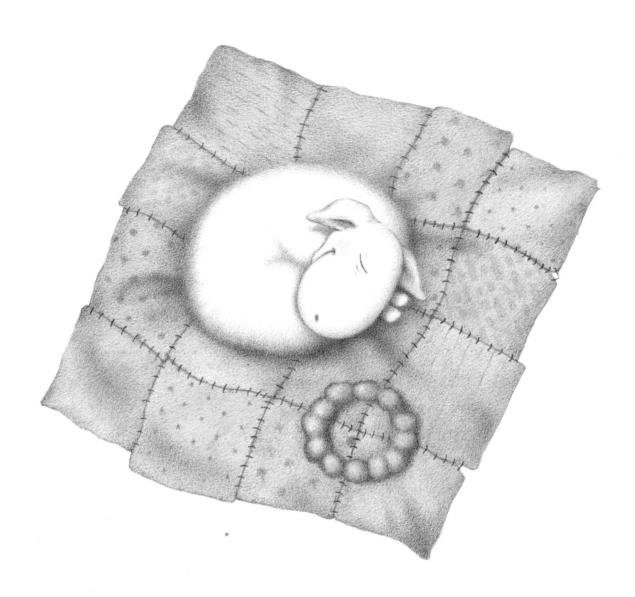

it was her very own.